GAYLORD F

The Sky Is Not So Far Away

The Sky Is Not So Far Away

Night Poems for Children

By
Margaret Hillert

Illustrated by
Thomas Werner

Wordsong / Boyds Mills Press

For Kathleen Balkema, a very special friend and
children's librarian. Dream true forever.
          —M. H.

To my father, William R. Werner, who taught me
the value of hard work.
          —T. W.

Text copyright © 1996 by Margaret Hillert
Illustrations copyright © 1996 by Boyds Mills Press
All rights reserved

Published by Wordsong
Boyds Mills Press, Inc.
A Highlights Company
815 Church Street
Honesdale, Pennsylvania 18431
Printed in Mexico

Publisher Cataloging-in-Publication Data
Hillert, Margaret.
    The sky is not so far away : night poems for children / by Margaret Hillert ;
illustrated by Thomas Werner.—1st ed.
[32]p. : col. ill. ; cm.
Summary : A collection of poems that captures the mystery and wonder of a
child's dreams.
ISBN 1-56397-223-9
1. Night—Juvenile Poetry. 2. Children's Poetry, American—Collections.
[1. Night—Poetry. 2. Poetry, American—Collections.] I. Werner, Thomas, ill.
II. Title.
811.54—dc20   1996   AC   CIP
Library of Congress Catalog Card Number 95-83167

First edition, 1996
Book designed by Jeffrey E. George
The text of this book is set in 16-point Caslon Roman.
The illustrations are done in watercolor.

10 9 8 7 6 5 4 3 2 1

CONTENTS

STARS

Why do people say *night falls*?
It never could. No, never.
It's fastened to the sky with stars
And should stay up forever.

NIGHT AT THE CIRCUS

We went to the circus.
We went to the circus.
We went to the CIRCUS
Last night.
The tent was so BIG,
And the noise was so LOUD,
And all of the colors
Were bright, bright, BRIGHT.

We saw
    Ladies on horseback
    And lions and tigers
    And acrobats swinging
    Way up in the air.

We saw
    Clowns turning cartwheels
    And seals flapping flippers,
    And right down in front
    Was a big dancing bear.

    I hardly could sleep,
    And I think when I'm grown,
    I'll start a big circus
    All of my own.

RAIN AT NIGHT

Sometimes the rain is very soft.
I hear it whisper from the sky.
The drip and drizzle from the roof
Is almost like a lullaby.
And all the world is getting wet,
But I am keeping warm and dry,
Snuggled down in my cozy bed
With Teddy Bear close by.

10

NIGHT CRAWLERS

Out on the lawn in the damp and the dark
We're flashing a light all around.
We're hunting for night crawlers here in the grass
For fishing tomorrow.

We found
A long skinny pink one, and two or three more
Just right for my bucket and pole,
But one got away as it wriggled and slid
Back down to a small muddy hole.

11

NIGHTTIME
AT THE BEACH

The tide is out.
The moon is bright,
And all the beach is silver white.
I hear the water lap the shore,
A gentle, whispered sound.
And I have found a special shell
And several magic stones as well
Here on this little mound.

But now the tide is getting higher.
My dad has made a roaring fire
And Mom has spread a rug.
She's getting out the food, I bet,
And so I'll hurry up to get
A hot dog and a hug.

LIGHTHOUSE

We see a lighthouse standing
Under the dark night sky.
It blinks a signal on and off
To help the ships pass by.
But sometimes when the fog is thick
And ships might run aground,
A foghorn adds its signal, too,
And moos a mournful sound.

14

MAYBE A MOUSE

At night—MAYBE—
There MIGHT be a mouse,
A brave little mouse,
A brown little mouse,
To scimper
And scamper
And run through the house
And sneeze a small sneeze
The right size for a mouse.

My dad wouldn't like it;
I'm quite sure of THAT.
My mom would be scared.
My sister'd scream "Rat!"
But I would be tickled
To know it was there,
So—MAYBE—one night
There MIGHT.

BEDTIME

It's bedtime,
And I'm all tucked in
With covers to my chin
And a kiss
And a hug.
But I think
I need another drink,
A little one, please,
And one more squeeze.

Sometimes it's lonely in the dark,
And scary.
Not very,
But some.
If I hold my teddy bear
And hum a little hum,
He'll feel all safe
And not be scared.
I'm glad we have each other.

A GOOD PLACE TO SLEEP

Little bear sleeps in the woods, in the woods.
Little gull sleeps on the sea.
Little colt sleeps in a big, big field.
Little squirrel sleeps in a tree.
Small fox sleeps in a den, in a den.
A hive is the place for a bee.
But here am I in my very own bed,
And that's the best place for me.

HIDE-AND-SEEK

It's nearly dark but not quite yet
So we can stay outside
For one more game of hide-and-seek.
The shadows help us hide.
I thought that you were near a bush
But when I went to see,
You raced from somewhere near the porch
And so you got in "free."
And now it's dark and I'm still IT
And there's no chance for me.

EXPRESSWAY
AT NIGHT

A dragon rushes through the night,
A dragon with a thousand eyes.
When truck horns blow or tires squeal
We sometimes hear its fearsome cries.
It wiggle-waggles down the road.
It roars along for mile on mile.
A steady stream of headlights makes
A mighty dragon for a while.

NIGHT SOUNDS

Sometimes I hear sirens.
Sometimes I hear snores.
Sometimes I hear footsteps
And slamming of doors.
Sometimes I hear purring.
Sometimes not a peep.
Sometimes I hear nothing—
Sometimes I'm asleep.

THE DREAM

I dreamed a birthday dream last night.
Balloons were everywhere.
And there were silly games to play
And funny hats to wear.
I dreamed a great big birthday cake
And lots of presents, too.
But best of all, when I woke up,
My dream was coming true!

NIGHT SNOW

Whitely, lightly, brightly,
Softly without sound,
Whirling, twirling, curling
Like feathers to the ground,
Blowing, glowing, growing
Higher flake by flake,
Piling up surprises
For the morning when I wake.

25

ICE-SKATING

We have a skating pond out back.
At night the ice is shiny black.
The moonlight through our cedar tree
Glows bright enough for us to see.
And so we skate and skate and skate,
And when Dad does a figure eight,
I do a one and zero.
THEN—
I win!
Because that makes a TEN!

KITTEN IN THE DARK

I pet my kitten in the dark
And sometimes see a little spark.
At other times when it is night,
Behind her eyes she lights a light.
And way down underneath her fur
I feel a rumbly kind of purr.
A motor runs inside her skin.
I wonder how she plugs it in.

MY TEDDY BEAR

A teddy bear is nice to hold.
The one I have is getting old.
His paws are almost wearing out
And so's his funny, furry snout
From rubbing on my nose of skin.
And all his fur is pretty thin.
A ribbon and a piece of string
Make a sort of necktie thing.
His eyes came out and now instead
He has some new ones made of thread.
I take him everywhere I go
And tell him all the things I know.
I like the way he feels at night,
All snuggled up against me tight.

NIGHT SHADOWS

When I'm outside, I run and play.
Our maple never moves all day.
But when night comes, it's strange to see
That somehow it has followed me.
I find its shadow on my wall,
Trunk and branches, leaves and all.
And somewhere in its shadows deep
There might be shadow birds asleep.

FIREWORKS

The night is in flower.
The night is in bloom
With blossoms of brightness
All over the sky.
I'm holding my ears
So I can't hear the BOOM!
I'm clapping my hands
As the fireworks fly.

NIGHT SKY

The sky is not so far away.
It reaches to the ground.
I'm standing right inside of it.
It doesn't make a sound.
And once I almost held a star,
A small and shining light
That turned into a firefly
And flickered out of sight.